JASON
AND THE GOLDEN FLEECE

Retold by
Claudia Zeff

Adapted by Gill Harvey

Illustrated by
Stephen Cartwright

Reading Consultant: Alison Kelly
University of Surrey Roehampton

Contents

Some pages show you how to say unusual names. The parts of the words in **bold** should be stressed.

Chapter 1

Wicked Uncle Pelias

Long ago in Greece, there lived a boy named Jason. He was supposed to become king of the island Iolcos*, but his Uncle Pelias* had stolen his throne.

When he was old enough, he set off to Iolcos to win it back.

* say ee-**ol**-cuss and **pee**-lee-ass

On the way, Jason carried an old woman across a river. As he waded through, he lost one of his sandals.

"Don't worry," said the woman. "If you go on with just one sandal, you'll become a great hero."

Then she disappeared. "How odd," thought Jason. But he did as she said, all the same.

When he got to Iolcos, his Uncle Pelias was not pleased to see him.

Uh-oh!
This spells trouble.

The gods had told him that a young man with only one sandal would come to take his throne.

"So, nephew!" sneered King Pelias. "You think I don't know why you've come? Well, I've a job for you first."

Jason wondered what he'd say. "Bring me the precious Golden Fleece, and the throne is yours!" the king said, with an evil smile.

Jason gulped. The Golden Fleece was far away in a place known as Colchis*. But he agreed.

He set to work right away. A man named Argus built him a ship. Then the goddess Athene* gave him a magic branch.

This will protect your ship.

Thank you, Athene.

* say **kol**-kiss and a-**thee**-nee

Jason named his ship the Argo. "Now, who shall I take with me?" he wondered.

Lots of people wanted to join the voyage. There was Orpheus*, who made wonderful music...

...Atlanta, a beautiful huntress, and Hercules*, the strongest man in the world.

Before long, Jason had almost fifty people who wanted to go. Then, with a flutter of wings, the North Wind's twin sons arrived.

"You're all fantastic!" said Jason. "Everyone can come."

Jason called his crew the Argonauts. They all piled onto the Argo for the long voyage.

With Athene's magic branch tied on tight, the Argo was ready to go.

The gods sent a gust of wind to fill the Argo's sail and the ship lurched forward. Jason and the Argonauts were off.

Chapter 2

Amycus the bully

After three days, the Argo stopped at an island. There was a big, hairy man on the beach... a *very* big man.

"I'm King Amycus*!" he roared. "Anyone who comes here has to fight me, or else!"

* say am-ic-us

One of the Argonauts stepped forward. "I am Polydeuces*. I'll fight you," he said bravely.

King Amycus laughed.

But Polydeuces wasn't scared. He went right up to the giant king. "I'm ready," he said calmly.

13

The Argonauts were worried, but they gathered around with the king's soldiers to watch the fight.

Amycus lunged at Polydeuces with his fat fists, but Polydeuces dodged. Amycus tried again, but Polydeuces was too fast for him.

Polydeuces ducked and darted for hours. As the sun sank lower in the sky, the king began to weaken.

Help! I can't see!

Cleverly, Polydeuces moved around so the sun shone straight into the king's eyes. Amycus was dazzled and stumbled.

Polydeuces grabbed his chance.
As the king tottered, he whacked
him on the head as hard as
he could.

That was the end of Amycus,
who dropped to the ground, dead.
His soldiers were very angry.

Jason and the Argonauts raced
to their ship and rowed away.

Chapter 3

The wise old man

As the Argonauts sailed on, a wild
and scary storm blew up. It
whipped up the waves and swept
the Argo onto a rocky island.

17

But the Argonauts were lucky. When the storm was over, they found that no one was hurt. The ship was fine, too.

"Let's explore the island," said Jason. He set off with two men from his crew. After a while, they found an old, spooky house.

18

They peeked around the door. Inside, it was dark and gloomy. Mice scuttled away from them, with squeaks of fear. "Hello?" they called. "Is anyone home?"

A blind man appeared at the top of the stairs. "Who's there?" he asked. He sounded tired.

Jason knew the old man at once. It was Phineas*, who could see into the future.

"Jason, with some friends," he called. "We're on a long journey. Can you tell us what dangers we will meet?"

One good turn deserves another...

"Only if you get rid of the Harpies," said Phineas. "They steal all my food."

20

* say **fin-ee-ass**

"OK," said Jason. "The sons of the North Wind can help."

As Phineas laid out some food, the Harpies came swooping down.

They were no match for the swift twins. Soon, all the Harpies were dead.

"At last!" cried Phineas in relief. "Thank you. Now, your greatest danger is the clashing rocks."

They might clash together and crush you.

"Take this dove. Let it go when you reach the rocks. If it flies through safely, you will be safe, too."

Chapter 4

Clashing rocks

The Argo set sail again and headed for the Black Sea.

The clashing rocks soon loomed ahead, dark and dangerous. Jason held up the dove and let it go.

The dove flew straight for the rocks. Jason watched as it dived between them.

"The rocks are clashing together!" he cried.

But then he saw the dove, safe on the other side. Just one white

feather fluttered down, where the rocks had trapped its tail.

24

"Let's go! Start rowing!" shouted Jason. But the wind was against them, and the rocks began to close together...

Faster! Faster!

The goddess Athene saw the danger and sent a wave to help them. The ship squeezed through, just in time.

The Argo sailed safely into the Black Sea. "Not far to go now," Jason told his crew.

But then they were attacked by some horrible birds, which shot poisoned arrows from their wings.

The crew fired arrows back, to scare them away.

The birds flew off in fright, and the Argo drew near to Colchis.

"We'll hide the Argo just outside Colchis," said Jason. "I'll visit the king in the morning."

Chapter 5

Challenge at Colchis

The next day, Jason went to find Aeetes*, the king of Colchis.

"I've come for the Golden Fleece," he explained.

"You can have it if you do the tasks I set for you," said Aeetes.

28

*say eye-**ee**-tees

Aeetes didn't want Jason to have the fleece at all. He had a cunning plan. "First, you must tame two bulls and use them to dig up a field," he said.

Then, you must sow the field with dragons' teeth.

Jason's heart sank. That sounded impossible! But he nodded bravely.

He had no idea how he would do it. He went back to his ship and talked to the Argonauts. None of them had any ideas, either.

What am I going to do?

But there was something that Jason didn't know. The king's daughter, Medea*, had seen him at the palace. She had fallen in love with him on the spot.

I must help Jason... but how?

Medea had heard her father set the impossible task. She was determined to help Jason.

31

* say meh-**dee**-ah

At last, she had an idea.
"Hecate*, the goddess of magic!"
Medea thought. "She'll help me."

In the dead of night, she drove
her chariot through the woods to
Hecate's temple.

There, she knelt in front of the
altar and pleaded with the goddess.

Please
tell me what to do,
Hecate!

Hecate told her to make a magic
potion with herbs from the woods.
"I'll do it now," said Medea.

With the potion made, Medea went to find Jason. He was in the woods, wandering by himself.

"Drink this," she whispered. "It's magic. It will protect you against the bulls."

Thank you for your help, princess.

All too soon, it was dawn. A crowd of people watched as Jason walked up to the bulls' cave.

Jason heard a loud bellow, then the thunder of the bulls' feet. As they ran, the ground shook. Jason took a deep breath.

Suddenly, the bulls charged at Jason, breathing fire. They had huge brass hooves and sharp, scary horns.

They scorched the ground near Jason with their fiery breath. But they didn't harm him.

"The potion's working!" thought Jason, in delight.

Slowly, Jason walked up to the monstrous bulls. The crowd held its breath. He grabbed their horns and forced them to kneel.

Then he stroked them and they snorted happily. The crowd gasped in disbelief.

"I'll get on with digging the field now," said Jason.

Jason soon finished digging the field. King Aeetes was furious.

"I've been tricked!" he fumed. He handed Jason a helmet full of dragons' teeth.

Jason marched up and down the field all day, sowing the teeth. By the time he had finished, the sun was beginning to set. Jason was very tired. It had been a long day.

Almost done.
But why would anyone want to sow dragons' teeth?

Jason went to the river for a drink of water, pleased he had finished. But suddenly, he heard shouting. He looked back.

Where he'd sown the teeth, soldiers were growing out of the ground!

This meant *real* trouble. What if they attacked everyone?

Jason thought quickly. He picked up a big stone and hurled it into the middle of the field.

Jason threw the stone so hard that it killed one of the soldiers.

"Who did that?" yelled the others.

Jason ducked down and hid.

The soldiers couldn't tell where the stone had come from. They shouted and argued.

Then they began to fight. It was a vicious, bloody battle. Soon most of the soldiers were dead.

Jason jumped up and killed the rest of the soldiers.

"Hurrah for Jason!" cheered the Argonauts. "He's our hero!"

Three cheers for Jason. Hip, hip, hooray!...

Medea was pleased, too, but she was afraid to show it. What if her father guessed her secret?

Chapter 6

The Golden Fleece

Aeetes was annoyed but he had one last task up his sleeve.

"You still have to fight the snake that guards the Golden Fleece," he told Jason. "I bet you can't do *that*."

But then, Aeetes began to worry.
What if Jason had magic powers?

"I'm not taking any chances,"
he said to himself. He called
his army.

Tonight,
you must burn the
Argo and kill all
her crew!

Medea overheard him.
She turned white and
rushed from the palace.

Medea ran all the way to the Argo. "Jason! Jason!" she called. "My father is plotting to burn your ship!"

"Hide the Argo," Jason ordered his crew hurriedly. Then he followed Medea into the woods.

Deep in the dark woods stood a massive oak tree. The Golden Fleece hung from its branches, glittering in the moonlight.

But the snake on guard was *vast*. Jason stared. It was the biggest snake he'd ever seen... as big as a dragon!

As Jason and Medea approached, the snake hissed and bared its fangs. Then it slithered up to them, its scales rattling.

"Don't worry," said Medea bravely. She began to sing.

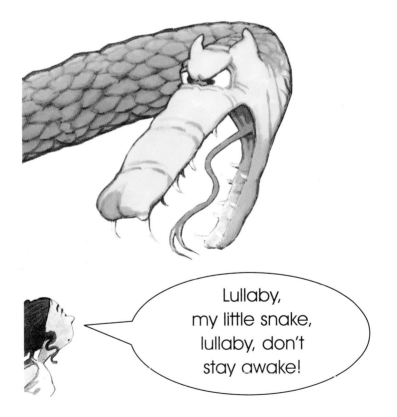

Lullaby, my little snake, lullaby, don't stay awake!

Slowly, the snake's eyes closed.
It was asleep.

Almost got it!

Jason scrambled up the tree and grabbed the fleece.

Jason and Medea rushed back to the Argo with the Golden Fleece. Jason held it up for the Argonauts to see.

"We have the fleece!" he cried. "Let's go!"

Quickly, the Argonauts set sail, taking Medea with them.

Chapter 7

A narrow escape

When Aeetes heard the news, he flew into a rage. "They won't get away with this!" he shouted.

He marched his army to the shore to board his fastest ships.

"After them!" cried Aeetes.

His small ships were much faster than the heavy Argo. By noon, they had almost caught up. Soon, the Argo was trapped.

"It's no use!" cried Jason. "There are too many of them. We'll have to give them the fleece." But Medea had an idea.

My brother Absyrtus is in charge of the ships.

"If we kill my brother, Absyrtus*, my father will give up," she said. "It's our only chance."

55

* say ab-**sir**-tus

"OK," said Jason. He called out to the king's ships. "Absyrtus, come aboard to make a truce!"

Too late, the men of Colchis realized what was happening. They watched helplessly as Medea stabbed her brother and threw him into the sea.

King Aeetes began to sob. "A curse upon Medea!" he wept.

King Aeetes ordered his men to fish Absyrtus out of the water. In the confusion, the Argo slipped away.

The king was too upset to chase Jason again. Sadly, he returned with his fleet to Colchis.

Chapter 8

King of Iolcos

Jason and Medea felt guilty for
what they had done. "Let's ask the
gods for forgiveness," said Medea.
So they stopped at the island home
of Circe*, a beautiful enchantress.

I am Circe.
Why have you
come?

* say **sir**-sea

"I killed my brother," Medea confessed. "Will the gods forgive me?"

Circe took them into her palace and waved her wand. There was a flash of light.

The gods have forgiven you!

"We can go home!" said Jason. He and Medea went back to the Argo and set sail happily.

When they reached Iolcos, Jason went straight to his uncle. "Here is the Golden Fleece!" he said. "Now, I want my throne back!"

I don't believe it!

King Pelias kept his word. Jason and Medea were married and crowned King and Queen of Iolcos.

The feasting and dancing lasted a month, celebrating the long-awaited return of Jason and his Argonauts.

Try these other books in **Series Two:**

Hercules: Hercules was the world's first superhero. But even superheroes have a hard time when faced with twelve impossible tasks.

King Arthur: Arthur is just a boy, until he pulls a sword out of a stone. Suddenly, he is King of England. The trouble is, not everyone wants him on the throne.

The Fairground Ghost: When Jake goes to the fair he wants a really scary ride. But first, he must teach the fairground ghost a trick or two.

The Amazing Adventures of Ulysses: Ulysses tries to rescue a princess and gets caught up in a ten-year war. Here, you can follow the story of his incredible voyage home.

Jason and the Golden Fleece was first written down in Ancient Greek about 2,200 years ago, by a poet named Apollonius of Rhodes. He wrote the story as a very long poem called *The Argonautica*.

Series Editor: Lesley Sims

Designed by
Katarina Dragoslavić

This edition first published in 2007 by Usborne Publishing Ltd., Usborne House, 83-85 Saffron Hill, London EC1N 8RT, England.
www.usborne.com
Copyright © 2007, 2003, 1982 Usborne Publishing Ltd.